Put Beginning Readers on the Right Track with ALL ABOARD READING™

The All Aboard Reading series is especially designed for beginning readers. Written by noted authors and illustrated in full color, these are books children really want to read—books to excite their imagination, expand their interests, make them laugh, and support their feelings. With fiction and nonfiction stories that are high interest and curriculum-related, All Aboard Reading books offer something for every young reader. And with four different reading levels, the All Aboard Reading series lets you choose which books are most appropriate for your children and their growing abilities.

Picture Readers
Picture Readers have super-simple texts, with many nouns appearing as rebus pictures. At the end of each book are 24 flash cards—on one side is a rebus picture; on the other side is the written-out word.

Station Stop 1
Station Stop 1 books are best for children who have just begun to read. Simple words and big type make these early reading experiences more comfortable. Picture clues help children to figure out the words on the page. Lots of repetition throughout the text helps children to predict the next word or phrase—an essential step in developing word recognition.

Station Stop 2
Station Stop 2 books are written specifically for children who are reading with help. Short sentences make it easier for early readers to understand what they are reading. Simple plots and simple dialogue help children with reading comprehension.

Station Stop 3
Station Stop 3 books are perfect for children who are reading alone. With longer text and harder words, these books appeal to children who have mastered basic reading skills. More complex stories captivate children who are ready for more challenging books.

In addition to All Aboard Reading books, look for All Aboard Math Readers™ (fiction stories that teach math concepts children are learning in school) and All Aboard Science Readers™ (nonfiction books that explore the most fascinating science topics in age-appropriate language).

All Aboard for happy reading!

For Morgie and Moffie's friends,
Dr. Cheryl and Dr. Ken Schunk and their staff
at the Hillsborough County Veterinary Hospital...
and for Mario who has never had a T-Rex missing!

Jennifer Smith-Stead, Literacy Consultant

Copyright © 2002 by Tomie dePaola. All rights reserved. Published by Grosset & Dunlap, a division of Penguin Young Readers Group, 345 Hudson Street, New York, NY 10014. GROSSET & DUNLAP, ALL ABOARD READING, and THE BARKER TWINS are trademarks of Penguin Group (USA) Inc. Published simultaneously in Canada. Printed in U.S.A.

Library of Congress Cataloging-in-Publication Data

De Paola, Tomie.
    T-rex is missing! / by Tomie dePaola.
        p. cm.
    Summary: Morgie accuses his best friend of taking his favorite dinosaur toy without asking, and then he finds that he must apologize.
    [1. Lost and found possessions—Fiction. 2. Dinosaurs—Fiction. 3. Toys—Fiction.
4. Friendship—Fiction.] I. Title.
PZ7.D439 Tr 2002
[E]—dc21
                                                                                        2002004661
ISBN 0-448-42870-9 (pbk)   F G H I J
ISBN 0-448-42882-2 (GB)   B C D E F G H I J

T-REX IS MISSING!

by Tomie dePaola

Grosset & Dunlap • New York

"Steggie, Steggie.

Come here," T-Rex said.

"Gotcha! It's my cave now."

"You mean <u>again</u>," Billy said.

"T-Rex always wins."

Billy asked,

"How come you are always T-Rex?"

"Because he's my favorite,"
Morgie answered.

Just then, Mama called Morgie.
"Come and get some snacks.
Billy has to go home soon."
"Okay, Mama," Morgie called.
"I'm coming."

Morgie came back.

Billy was packing up his backpack.

They had snacks.

Then Billy went home.

After dinner,

Morgie got ready for bed.

He counted his dinosaurs.

Oh, no! T-Rex was missing!

Morgie looked all over—
under the bed,

in the cave,

and behind the bookcase.

"I bet Billy took T-Rex home,"
Morgie said.
"And he didn't ask me!"

The next morning,

Morgie saw Billy.

"Where's T-Rex?" Morgie asked.

"I don't know," Billy said.

"I don't have him."

"Well, you better give him back,"
Morgie said.

And he walked away.

Morgie was mad at Billy.

Billy was mad at Morgie.

They didn't sit together

at story time.

They didn't play catch together.

They didn't share lunch.

They didn't even say good-bye!

"Why are you and Billy in a fight?"
Moffie asked.

"None of your business,"
Morgie snapped.

"Well, excuse me!" Moffie said.

"How was your day?"
Mama asked the twins.
"Morgie and Billy had a fight,"
Moffie said.

Mama said,
"Well, I am sure they will make up
and be friends again."

Morgie went outside.

"Want to go on the swing?"

Morgie asked Marcos.

"No, gracias. No, thank you,"

his little brother said.

Morgie went inside.

"Want to play dinosaurs?"
Morgie asked Moffie.

"No, thank you," Moffie said.

Morgie felt all alone.

He went to his room.

There on his bed was T-Rex!

Morgie hugged T-Rex.

"Where were you?"

Morgie asked.

Mama heard Morgie.

"I found T-Rex in Marcos's room.

He slept with T-Rex last night."

Oh, no! thought Morgie.
Billy didn't take T-Rex
after all.

At dinner,

Morgie told everybody

the whole story.

"Well," Papa said,

"you need to tell Billy

you are sorry."

Mama nodded.

"Then you will be friends again."

Morgie nodded.

This was going to be hard!

The next morning,
the twins saw Billy.
"Morgie has something to tell you,"
Moffie said.

"I'm sorry, Billy," Morgie said.

He told Billy everything.

"I feel really bad.

Can we be friends again?"

"Sure," Billy said.

It was after school.

Morgie and Billy were playing

with Morgie's dinosaurs.

"Gotcha!" Billy yelled.

"It's my cave now!"

Morgie and Billy laughed.